FAVOURITE NURSERY RHYMES

....

....

....

....

This edition first published in Picture Lions in 1999.

1 3 5 7 9 10 8 6 4 2

ISBN 0 00 664698-0

Picture Lions is an imprint of the Children's Division,
part of HarperCollins Publishers Ltd,
77-85 Fulham Palace Road, Hammersmith, London W6 8JB.
The HarperCollins website address is www.fireandwater.com

Illustrations this edition © Jonathan Langley 1996
Compilation this edition © HarperCollins Publishers 1999

Printed and bound in Singapore by Imago

FAVOURITE NURSERY RHYMES

Illustrated by Jonathan Langley

PictureLions
An Imprint of HarperCollins*Publishers*

CONTENTS

Jack and Jill
Went up the hill,
To fetch a pail of water;
Jack fell down,
And broke his crown,
And Jill came tumbling after.

Baa, baa, black sheep,
Have you any wool?
Yes, sir, yes, sir,
Three bags full;
One for the master,
And one for the dame,
And one for the little boy
Who lives down the lane.

Mary had a little lamb,
Its fleece was white as snow;
And everywhere that Mary went
The lamb was sure to go.

It followed her to school one day,
That was against the rule;
It made the children laugh and play
To see a lamb at school.

Humpty Dumpty sat on a wall,
Humpty Dumpty had a great fall.
All the king's horses
And all the king's men
Couldn't put Humpty together again.

Old King Cole
Was a merry old soul,
And a merry old soul was he;
He called for his pipe,
And he called for his bowl,
And he called for his fiddlers three.

Every fiddler he had a fiddle,
And a very fine fiddle had he;
Oh, there's none so rare
As can compare
With King Cole and his fiddlers three.

There was an old woman who lived in a shoe.
She had so many children she didn't know what to do.
She gave them some broth without any bread.
She spanked them all soundly and put them to bed.

There was a crooked man, and he walked a crooked mile,
He found a crooked sixpence against a crooked stile;
He bought a crooked cat, which caught a crooked mouse,
And they all lived together in a little crooked house.

Old Mother Hubbard
Went to the cupboard,
To fetch her poor dog a bone.
When she got there,
The cupboard was bare,
And so the poor dog had none.

Little Miss Muffet
Sat on a tuffet,
Eating her curds and whey;
There came a big spider,
Who sat down beside her
And frightened Miss Muffet away.

One, two,
Buckle my shoe;
Three, four,
Knock at the door;
Five, six,
Pick up sticks;
Seven, eight,
Lay them straight;
Nine, ten,
A big fat hen;

Eleven, twelve,
Dig and delve;
Thirteen, fourteen,
Maids a-courting;
Fifteen, sixteen,
Maids in the kitchen;
Seventeen, eighteen,
Maids in waiting;
Nineteen, twenty,
My plate's empty.

Little Bo-Peep has lost her sheep,
And doesn't know where to find them;
Leave them alone, and they'll come home
Bringing their tails behind them.

Then up she took her little crook
Determined for to find them;
She found them indeed, but it made her heart bleed,
For they'd left all their tails behind them.

It happened one day, as Bo-Peep did stray
Into a meadow hard by:
There she espied their tails side by side,
All hung on a tree to dry.

She heaved a sigh, and wiped her eye
And over the hillocks went rambling,
And tried what she could,
    as a shepherdess should,
To tack again each to its lambkin.

The Queen of Hearts,
She made some tarts,
All on a summer's day.
The Knave of Hearts,
He stole the tarts,
And took them clean away.

The King of Hearts
Called for the tarts,
And beat the Knave full sore.
The Knave of Hearts
Brought back the tarts
And vowed he'd steal no more.

"Oranges and lemons," say the bells of St Clement's.
"You owe me five farthings," say the bells of St Martin's.
"When will you pay me?" say the bells of Old Bailey.
"When I grow rich," say the bells of Shoreditch.
"Pray when will that be?" say the bells of Stepney.
"I'm sure I don't know," says the great bell of Bow.

Here comes the candle to light you to bed,
And here comes a chopper to chop
off your head.

Chip chop, chip chop,
The last man's head.

Half a pound of tuppenny rice,
Half a pound of treacle,
That's the way the money goes,
Pop goes the weasel!

Up and down the city road,
In and out the eagle,
That's the way the money goes,
Pop goes the weasel!

Every night when I go out,
The monkey's on the table,
Take a stick and knock it off,
Pop goes the weasel!

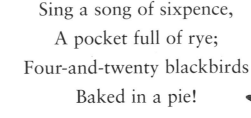

Sing a song of sixpence,
A pocket full of rye;
Four-and-twenty blackbirds
Baked in a pie!

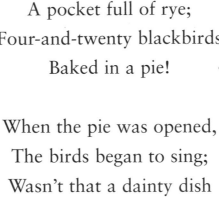

When the pie was opened,
The birds began to sing;
Wasn't that a dainty dish
To set before the king?

The king was in his counting-house
Counting out his money;
The queen was in the parlour,
Eating bread and honey.

The maid was in the garden,
Hanging out the clothes;
When down came a blackbird
And pecked off her nose.

Oh, the grand old Duke of York,
He had ten thousand men;
He marched them up
To the top of the hill,
And he marched them down again.

And when they were up, they were up,
And when they were down, they were down,
And when they were only halfway up,
They were neither up nor down.

This little piggy went to market;
This little piggy stayed at home;
This little piggy had roast beef;
This little piggy had none;
And this little piggy cried, "Wee! Wee! Wee!"
All the way home.

Round and round the garden,
Goes the Teddy Bear,
One step,
Two step,
Tickle you under there!

Five currant buns in a baker's shop,
Round and fat with sugar on the top.
Along came a boy with a penny one day,
Bought a currant bun and took it away.

Down by the station, early in the morning,
See the little puffer trains all in a row.
See the engine driver pull the little handle.
Choo, choo, choo, and off we go.

Down at the farmyard early in the morning,
See the little tractor standing in the barn.
Do you see the farmer pull the little handle?
Chug, chug, chug, and off we go.

Hey diddle, diddle,
The cat and the fiddle,
The cow jumped over the moon;
The little dog laughed to see such sport,
And the dish ran away with the spoon.

Georgy Porgy, pudding and pie,
Kissed the girls and made them cry.
When the boys came out to play,
Georgy Porgy ran away.

Twinkle, twinkle, little star,
How I wonder what you are!
Up above the world so high,
Like a diamond in the sky.

When the blazing sun is gone,
When he nothing shines upon,
Then you show your little light,
Twinkle, twinkle, all the night.

Then the traveller in the dark,
Thanks you for your tiny spark,
He could not see which way to go,
If you did not twinkle so.

In the dark blue sky you keep,
And often through my curtains peep,
For you never shut your eye,
Till the sun is in the sky.

As your bright and tiny spark,
Lights the traveller in the dark –
Though I know not what you are,
Twinkle, twinkle, little star.

Hickory, dickory, dock,
The mouse ran up the clock.
The clock struck one,
The mouse ran down,
Hickory, dickory, dock.

Wee Willie Winkie runs through the town,
Upstairs and downstairs in his nightgown,
Rapping at the window, crying through the lock,
"Are all the children in their beds, it's now eight o'clock?"

Rock-a-bye, Baby, on the tree top;
When the wind blows, the cradle will rock;
When the bough bends, the cradle will fall;
Down will come baby, cradle and all.